For Mother Placid, O.S.B.,
who taught ME to sing,

and the Benedictine Community
of the Abbey of Regina Laudis
in Bethlehem, Connecticut

G. P. PUTNAM'S SONS
A division of Penguin Young Readers Group.
Published by The Penguin Group.
Penguin Group (USA) Inc., 375 Hudson Street, New York, NY 10014, U.S.A.
Penguin Group (Canada), 90 Eglinton Avenue East, Suite 700, Toronto, Ontario M4P 2Y3, Canada
(a division of Pearson Penguin Canada Inc.).
Penguin Books Ltd, 80 Strand, London WC2R 0RL, England.
Penguin Ireland, 25 St. Stephen's Green, Dublin 2, Ireland (a division of Penguin Books Ltd.).
Penguin Group (Australia), 250 Camberwell Road, Camberwell, Victoria 3124, Australia
(a division of Pearson Australia Group Pty Ltd).
Penguin Books India Pvt Ltd, 11 Community Centre, Panchsheel Park, New Delhi - 110 017, India.
Penguin Group (NZ), 67 Apollo Drive, Rosedale, North Shore 0632, New Zealand (a division of Pearson New Zealand Ltd).
Penguin Books (South Africa) (Pty) Ltd, 24 Sturdee Avenue, Rosebank, Johannesburg 2196, South Africa.
Penguin Books Ltd, Registered Offices: 80 Strand, London WC2R 0RL, England.

Library of Congress Cataloging-in-Publication Data
De Paola, Tomie.
The song of Francis / Tomie dePaola.   p. cm.
Summary: Francis, the Little Poor One, is so filled with the love of God that he bursts into song, and he is joined by
birds of every color.   [1. Color—Fiction. 2. Christian life—Fiction. 3. Francis, of Assisi, Saint 1182–1226—Fiction.]
I. Title.   PZ7.D439Sm 2009   [E]—dc22   2008018578

ISBN 978-0-399-25210-5
10 9 8 7 6 5 4 3 2 1

Tomie dePaola

THE SONG OF FRANCIS

G. P. Putnam's Sons

Francis was so filled with the love of God
that he wanted to sing,
to tell everyone how much God loved them.

But he was all alone.

Except for a small angel
who followed him everywhere.

"Little Poor One," the angel whispered in his ear,
"sing anyway. The loving God will hear you.
And so will I."

So Francis began to sing.

"Sun and Moon, bless the Lord,
for the Lord loves you."
Brother Sun was shining,

but Sister Moon came into the sky too,
because she wanted to
hear the song as well.

"Birds of the air," Francis sang,

"come and bless the Lord,
because the Lord loves you."

And one by one, birds came to sit in the tree
to hear Francis sing.

Red birds,
orange birds,
yellow birds,
green birds,
blue birds,
violet birds,
brown birds,
black birds,
and white birds.

They all began to join
Francis, the Little Poor One,
in the song.

A more glorious sound—
a more glorious sight was
never seen on the earth before.

So angels came to see and to listen.

"Love, love, love," went the song.

Then Francis was silent.
His song was over.

The angels left, one by one, to go back to heaven.

The birds left, one by one,
to go back to the sky.

the yellow birds,

the orange birds,

the blue birds,

the green birds,

The white birds,

the black birds,

the brown birds,

the violet birds,

the red birds,
one by one.

Then Brother Sun left the sky,

but Sister Moon stayed to light the path,
because it had turned to night.

Then Francis, the Little Poor One,
was alone again, except for the small angel
who followed him everywhere.

"Tomorrow," he whispered to the angel,
"I shall sing again."